PLUM BLOSSOM MEDIA

WIDDLE
AND WADDLE
CREATE THE PINWHEEL TOY

Mary Fey

ISBN 978-1-64468-270-8 (Paperback)
ISBN 978-1-64468-271-5 (Hardcover)
ISBN 978-1-64468-272-2 (Digital)

Copyright © 2020 Mary Fey
All rights reserved
First Edition

All rights reserved. No part of this publication may be reproduced, distributed, or transmitted in any form or by any means, including photocopying, recording, or other electronic or mechanical methods without the prior written permission of the publisher. For permission requests, solicit the publisher via the address below.

Covenant Books, Inc.
11661 Hwy 707
Murrells Inlet, SC 29576
www.covenantbooks.com

To all who are seeking to walk close with Jesus and
to my beloved Edward, the love of my life!

1

Widdle and Waddle were a very industrious crew…
they worked and they worked, till they saw the job through.

Their town had been the cutest little place.
But hard times had come, and now it was a disgrace!

They arose early every morning, and they tried to see
new ideas they would ponder, under a hickory nut tree.

They thought about the beautiful
forest, just outside of town.
At a town meeting someone suggested, they cut it all down!

The mayor said, "I'm just thinking it would make jobs.
It's too bad the factory closed down that makes doorknobs.

3

"You all must think I'm some kind of jerk!"
"That is not true, said Waddle. "We all need work."

"Yes!" said the mayor. "My children are
running out of hand-me-downs.
We need new businesses to stop this town
from having more shutdowns."

Widdle said, "Cutting down the trees
is an idea I want to resist.
When they are gone, we have less instead
of more, if you get my gist."

Other people joined with Widdle and
Waddle to a big thumbs down!
The mayor said, "We will think of
something, or I will step down.

"Right now we need to help each
other, so we can all coexist.
Can we pull together? I for one am going to persist!

"It would be great if we could come
up with a total new twist.
Maybe some of you could improve on
something that already exists!"

"Don't worry we will find something
to put this town on the map.
When that happens prosperity will
be sitting in everyone's lap!"

The next morning Widdle and Waddle
took a walk through town.
They saw a new sign that said, "Last markdown!"

"Looks to me like half the town is out of work.
We are going to have to do some fancy footwork!"

So then they walked through the woods.
Can you guess what they found?
There were all these little sticks that covered the ground.

They had gathered some sticks and put them in a pile
so they could come back for them after a while.

"Look how many we have," said Widdle with disbelief.
"I was so busy I didn't notice," said Waddle. "Good grief!"

"These sticks are still just sticks," said Widdle with unbelief.
"Wait! I have an idea," said Waddle.
"How about adding a leaf?"

Waddle looked for different-shaped leaves
and found some that were just fine.
"What a great idea," said Widdle. "I wish it were mine!"

He fastened some leaves on the end of each stick.
Then the wind blew, and they spun around quite quick.

8

"Look what you've done," said Widdle.
"You have invented a toy!
Let's go show everybody, especially every girl and boy."

"It is time to call another town meeting.
This time we can give them a very happy greeting!"

Widdle explained the idea to the
people and was very profound.
Then Waddle, whose idea it was, continued to expound.

Widdle had started wittling, so fast that Waddle could see.
Then he said, "Wow! You won't get ahead of me!

"I was ready to lodge a complaint!
Because Waddle had made all my sticks
wet with slow drying paint!"

"I want to thank you," the mayor of the town said.
"Widdle, you are one remarkable fellow!"

"Not me," said Widdle. "It was Waddle's idea
to paint the sticks pink, green, and yellow!

"Matter of fact, a light bulb was about
to go off above his head.
My brother was about to come up with an idea
that would have knocked mine dead!"

"Wow!" said a man. "You have come
up with a wonderful thing.
With all the bright colors…it gives it a real zing!

"Let's get started. This is an idea we must not postpone.
How far we can go with this is completely unknown.

13

14

"To give everyone a job is first on our list.
We can expect spectacular results, if you get my gist!

"When can we get started? We are all close to being broke.
Can we start tomorrow?"
Widdle looked at Waddle and said, "Okeydoke.

"Who can help me wittle sticks at day's first light?
Second shift can help Waddle paint into the night.

"This is a wonderful thing that has happened…
At last we had work that the whole town could pursue."
Everyone was so happy…this was like a dream come true.

"We will attach it to the children's bicycle bars…
We will attach it to the grown people's cars.

"This is the latest prettiest toy.
That will bring many children great joy!

"When you have a child just running around,
it just makes a very sweet sound.

"But when you put it on a car,
the sound travels very far."

Widdle and Waddle had invented the pinwheel!
They were passing them around…
Each child received a pinwheel and
was off to the playground!

As word spread around about the
factory fun, people would come
from far and wide to see the pinwheels run.

They would pass by the fountain at the entrance of town
that when things went wrong was completely shut down.

What was just a fountain, ha-ha, at the
base a very small lake, it is now so very
beautiful. It looks like a wedding cake!

Once a year there is a Pinwheel Fair!

To do this, the whole town takes such care to make
sure that each display is done with a lot of flair.

They built a cafe on top of the factory.
That is just hunky-dory.
When the visitors come by, well, it
just tells the whole story!

From the roof of the cafe everyone can see…where
the idea was born under the hickory nut tree.

HOW MANY?

1. Dogs
2. Ice-cream cones
3. Restaurant tables
4. Soda glasses
5. Pinwheel on baseball caps
6. Straw hats
7. Pinwheels on hats
8. Pigtails you can see
9. Balloons
10. Pinwheels on animals
11. Ponytails
12. Different animals
13. Signs (not real people)
14. Babies
15. Having their picture taken
16. Scooters
17. Pinwheel pictures on T-shirts

ANSWER KEY

1) 7
2) 2
3) 5
4) 13
5) 3
6) 3
7) 5
8) 3
9) 2
10) 3
11) 1
12) 3
13) 2
14) 1
15) 2
16) 1
17) 2

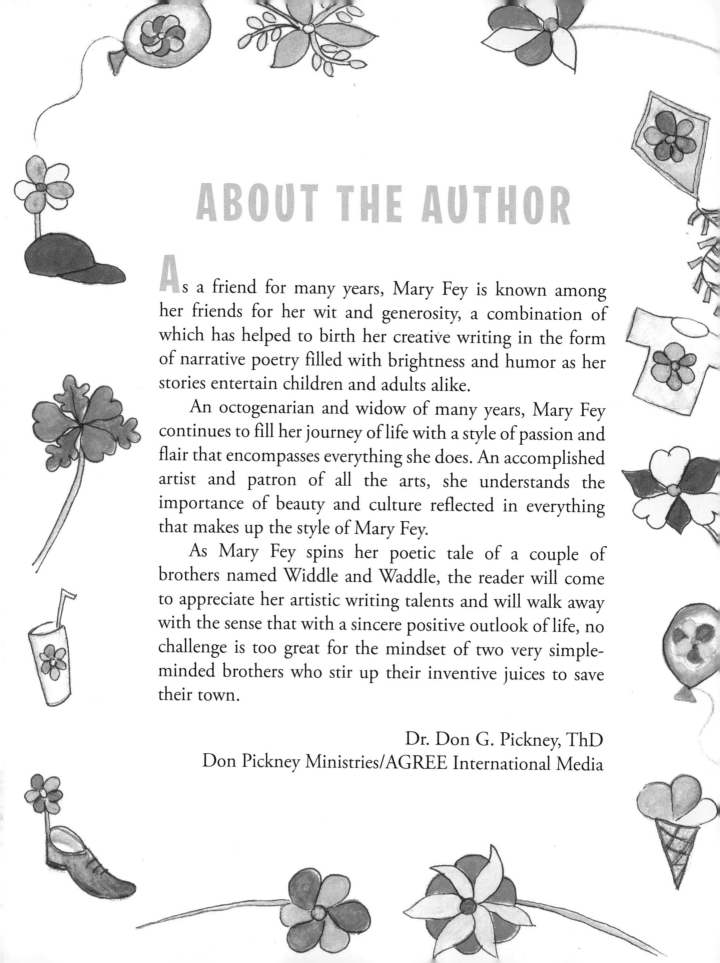

ABOUT THE AUTHOR

As a friend for many years, Mary Fey is known among her friends for her wit and generosity, a combination of which has helped to birth her creative writing in the form of narrative poetry filled with brightness and humor as her stories entertain children and adults alike.

An octogenarian and widow of many years, Mary Fey continues to fill her journey of life with a style of passion and flair that encompasses everything she does. An accomplished artist and patron of all the arts, she understands the importance of beauty and culture reflected in everything that makes up the style of Mary Fey.

As Mary Fey spins her poetic tale of a couple of brothers named Widdle and Waddle, the reader will come to appreciate her artistic writing talents and will walk away with the sense that with a sincere positive outlook of life, no challenge is too great for the mindset of two very simple-minded brothers who stir up their inventive juices to save their town.

Dr. Don G. Pickney, ThD
Don Pickney Ministries/AGREE International Media

CPSIA information can be obtained
at www.ICGtesting.com
Printed in the USA
JSHW040024220720
6793JS00003B/38

9 781644 682708